Generation OF THE Gods

KEONA KING

GENERATIONS

OF THE

GODS

GIFTED TO:

_____

FROM:

_____

DEDICATION

I want to dedicate the biggest thanks to my mother, who read a middle school project and saw pure potential (and also did not let me rest until I'd tapped into it).

My mom spent many hours rereading and revising with me, making the process of writing my first book—and many more to come—so much more enjoyable. She has been my biggest supporter through everything and is always excited to see me try to excel at something new.

I would also like to thank my editor, who dedicated her time to editing this book so that it could be published. Thank you; you are appreciated!

And lastly, thank you guys! Thank you to all my readers for choosing this book as your next adventure. Thank you for your curiosity and for giving my art a chance. I hope you all get to experience the excitement I felt while writing it!

Keona King

FOREWORD

In every generation, some stories echo timeless truths, tales that remind us of where we come from, who we are, and the divine purpose that calls us higher.

Generations of the Gods by *Keona King* is one such book. Though fictional in form, its pages are rich with moral depth, spiritual wisdom, and reflections that mirror the journey of every human soul searching for meaning in a world that's constantly shifting.

In this collection, *Keona* does more than tell stories; she builds bridges between her personal experiences and the modern world we live in —the sacred and the everyday.

Each narrative invites readers to confront life's most profound questions: Who am I? Why am I here?

Through her characters' struggles, victories, and transformations, *Keona* gently leads us toward a central truth that no matter how advanced or enlightened we believe our generation has become, the need for a genuine relationship with God remains unchanged.

This book is more than entertainment; it's a spiritual mirror. It calls us to remember that divine connection is not an option; it is the foundation of identity, peace, and destiny. *Generations of the Gods* challenges us to rediscover that foundation and to pass it on to the next generation.

Prepare to be inspired, challenged, and awakened. These stories may be fictional, but the lessons they reveal are real and eternal.

Dr. Wilfred Brown,
President,
Motivating Youth Impacting Lives Foundation "MYIL"

TABLE OF CONTENTS

CHAPTER ONE

The Boarder

PART 1

Still Here

The wind over **Floom City** hit different at night. Not cold—just sharp, like it knew exactly where to slice you open if you stood still too long.

I sat on the rusted edge of our building's rooftop, sneakers kicking against the cracked billboard frame underneath me. Below, a neon ocean of light buzzed and pulsed: hovercars weaved through sky lanes, storefronts flickered in outdated LED, and down at street level, the bassline of the city never stopped. **Floom** never slept. It just changed masks.

Me? I hadn't slept much since last year. Since the crash.

The city didn't care, of course. It didn't pause for grief. It didn't notice when the last thing holding you together came apart. It just kept moving. You had to figure out how to move with it—or disappear under it.

I didn't disappear. I just stopped being someone worth seeing.

My name is **Callum**. I'm sixteen. And if the world ended tomorrow, I doubt my name would show up on any *"Remember When"* list unless the future loves dramatic, half-broken teenagers who can't do math and spend too much time on rooftops.

I used to skateboard every day. It was my thing. Since I was three, I'd skate circles around adults, flip tricks off hydrants, and launch myself off garage roofs. People used to yell at me— *"That kid's gonna break his neck!"* Maybe they were right.

After the accident, though, I quit. I told myself I had to *"grow up."* Whatever that meant. **Jax**—my brother—he didn't ask me to. Nobody did. I just thought it was what grown-ups did when they were grieving. They cut out the parts that make life worth living.

But here's the thing: people didn't stop calling me "**The Boarder.**" Even without the board. The name stuck like a scar. I'd walk down the hall at school and hear it whispered: *"There goes the boarder."* As if I was still gliding past lockers, hoodie flapping, music billowing from my backpack like smoke from one of the city's many factories.

Funny how people hold onto labels long after you've dropped them.

PART 2

Bus Ride with Dorian

"You're doing it again," Dorian said.

I blinked and realized I'd been staring at the same scratch on the bus window for what had to be five stops.

"What?" I ask as though nothing had happened.

She leaned closer, resting her chin on the edge of the torn vinyl seat in front of me, one eyebrow raised and ready to launch a lecture. "That thing where you leave your body and float off into the **Sad Boy Cinematic Universe.**"

"Sorry," I muttered. "I was thinking."

"Oh no. That's dangerous."

Her voice had that theatrical *lilt*[1] she always used when she was trying to make a point sound like a joke, even when it wasn't. I turned slightly, giving her the most minuscule smirk I

---

[1] Lilt – a light, rhythmic, and pleasant rise and fall in the sound of a voice or tune. Source: Google Definition.

could manage without betraying effort.

"You ever think maybe I'm just quiet sometimes?" I asked.

She laughed—a short, bright noise that made two younger kids in the back glance up. "No. You're not quiet. You're plotting. Or spiraling. Sometimes both."

"I'm not spiraling," I retorted.

"You're wearing the same hoodie for the third day in a row, your shoelace is literally *hanging on for life* with a paperclip, and you've been staring down that crack like it owes you money."

I looked down, but couldn't help but smirk. Yeah, okay, she had me on the paperclip.

She bumped her shoulder against mine. "Come on, **Callum**. You've got the tragic backstory, the angsty[2] vibe, the mysterious nickname—people would pay to be you."

"Yeah," I muttered. "Too bad I'm not for sale."

Her grin faltered. Just a fraction. She caught it herself and switched gears.

---

[2] Angsty – to experience or express angst, which is a feeling of deep anxiety, apprehension, or insecurity, often mixed with frustration and negativity. Source: Google Definition.

"You know what you need?" she said, pulling a stick of gum from her pocket like a magician producing a rabbit. "A reboot. New hobby. A distraction."

"You are my distraction."

"That's the nicest thing you've ever said to me," she deadpanned. "I'm tearing up."

I took the gum and chewed silently, the mint sharp against the back of my throat.

She let the quiet settle for a few blocks before nudging me again. "You should write it."

"Write what?"

"All this," she said, gesturing toward me like I was some half-finished science project. "The whole thing. The crash. The silence. The blue hoodies and late-night rooftop monologues."

I rolled my eyes. "That would be the most boring book ever written."

"Not if you actually did something," she said, sharper than I expected. "Not if you stopped just floating through it."

I didn't answer. The bus *hissed* to a stop. I stood, slung my bag over one shoulder.

"Let a man spiral in peace," I said flatly.

She sighed. "No one writes stories about people who disappear, **Callum**."

I stepped off the bus and let the door close between us.

PART 3

The Call

The living room hadn't changed in months. Blank walls. One couch, half-sunk. A broken lamp we still hadn't replaced. My drum kit in the corner, untouched. I eyed it for a second before turning away.

My phone buzzed. Once. Then again.

I reached for it lazily, thumb swiping across the cracked screen.

Incoming call: Nurse Joy

I blinked, a suspicious eyebrow quirking at the sight. That wasn't right.

She never called me first.

Ever.

Even when I skipped check-ins, forgot my refills, or told

her I was *"fine"* through clenched teeth, she never initiated. That was our rule. I called her. Never the other way around.

I answered before the third ring.

"Hello?"

"Callum?"

Her voice was tight. Not panicked, but restrained. Like she was trying not to panic.

"Hey, Nurse Joy. Is everything okay?"

A pause.

"Not with **Jax.***"*

I didn't hear the rest of what she said. Something about a bike. An intersection. Paramedics.

My ears filled with a sound I hadn't heard since the day they told me my parents weren't coming home—like a gunshot echoing inside my skull, again and again. My chest tightened. Not fear. Not grief.

Static.

I dropped the phone.

It hit the carpet with a thud that felt louder than anything

I'd heard all day.

PART 4

Lights Out

The room didn't tilt or spin. That would've been too dramatic. It just dropped.

As if gravity got tired of holding me up and decided I wasn't worth the effort anymore.

I barely made it to the couch before my knees gave out. I sat there, palms on my thighs, staring at nothing. The hum of the city leaked in through the windows. Traffic, low music, distant voices. It all sounded like it was coming from behind a wall of glass.

My hands were shaking. My breath wouldn't settle. My brother—my last actual person—was lying somewhere with machines around him and strangers trying to keep him from going where my parents already went.

I tried to blink. Something stung.

I stood up. Or maybe I just floated. It was hard to tell.

I walked toward the shelf near the kitchen—the one with the pictures. I don't even know why. Maybe I wanted to see their faces again. Or perhaps I needed proof I ever had a family to lose in the first place.

There was one photo I never liked. The three of us. Jax's arm over my shoulder. Mom and Dad were behind us, both wearing matching fleece jackets they thought were cute. I was twelve. It was one of the last normal days.

The glass in the frame was cracked from when I dropped it months ago. I never replaced it.

I stared at it, blurry-eyed, until something flickered.

A glow.

Not in the frame.

In me.

I leaned closer, squinting. In the reflection, my eyes weren't my eyes.

They were lit up—*glowing*, a dim bluish sheen pulsing just beneath the surface. The light wasn't intense. It didn't feel like a flashlight. It felt like something alive, trying to crawl out.

My fingers twitched.

Then my knees buckled.

I hit the floor hard—cheek against carpet, vision doubling, a crack of pain blooming in my head.

And then, everything folded in.

No sound. No light. No time.

Just cold blue silence.

PART 5

Blue Glow

The beeping came first. Steady, slow. Like a metronome[3] trying to calm me down.

Then the smell—sterile, artificial, lemony. The unmistakable scent of hospitals. I hated that smell. It always reminded me of things I desperately wished I could bury.

I cracked my eyes open.

Everything was too white. Walls, sheets, ceiling. It felt like I had fallen into a snow globe. A very dull, overly lit snow globe.

Nurse **Joy** sat beside the bed, arms crossed over her clipboard. Her face softened the second she saw me.

---

[3] Metronome — a device that produces a regular, audible, or visual pulse to help musicians maintain a consistent tempo and rhythm, often measured in beats per minute (BPM.) Source: Google Definition.

"**Callum**," she said, half-relieved, half-scolding. "You're awake."

I blinked. "How'd I get here?"

"You passed out. Hit your head. Your neighbor found you on the floor when you didn't answer the door. He called emergency services." She leaned forward slightly. "You scared everyone. Again."

I looked away.

There was an IV in my arm. A bandage on my temple. Machines next to the bed with wires snaking toward my chest.

"I'm fine," I muttered.

"No, you're not." Her voice was gentle, but firm. "And I know you stopped taking your medication months ago."

I didn't answer.

She sighed and shook her head. "I'm not here to scold you. But you can't keep doing this alone."

I wanted to say *I wasn't trying to*. But the words wouldn't come. I knew they weren't true.

She glanced at the monitor, scribbled something, then stood. "You're stable now. They'll discharge you tonight. Your brother's okay, by the way—minor injuries. He'll be home by morning."

Relief hit so fast it almost hurt. Like I'd been holding my breath for hours without realizing it.

She left the room, soft-soled shoes clicking against linoleum.

I exhaled and stared at the ceiling. Just me again.

Except…

There was a sound. A low, faint hum. Not from the machines.

From me.

I looked down at my hand. The one not attached to any tubes.

Tiny blue wisps curled around my fingertips, faint and flickering, like smoke made of light. They pulsed once, like a heartbeat.

And then disappeared.

Just enough to make me question if I'd seen them at all.

CHAPTER TWO

The Fall and the Flame

PART 1

Cracked Glass

Two months earlier.

"You can't just keep hiding in here, Callum."

Jax's voice echoed off the kitchen walls, cutting through the early autumn heat that hadn't yet figured out it was supposed to leave. His arms were crossed, eyes heavy with that look I hated—the one that said I'm your brother, but I'm also the only adult left, so this is what we're doing now.

I stood by the sink, gripping a cracked glass like it owed me an answer.

"I'm not hiding," I muttered.

Jax scoffed. "Really? Because from where I'm standing, you haven't left this apartment in three days. You haven't skated. You haven't showered. You skipped your sessions with

Joy again—"

"I didn't skip," I interrupted. "I rescheduled."

"To when? The next apocalypse?"

The silence that followed wasn't dramatic. It was worn out. Tired. Like the pause in a song you've played too many times.

I stared at the water swirling down the drain. "You don't get it."

"I don't get it?" **Jax** stepped closer. "**Callum,** I was there. I held your hand at the hospital. I sat through the funeral. I'm still trying to keep both of us afloat while you float off into space every time someone says something real."

"I'm sixteen," I said. "I'm allowed to fall apart."

He sighed, rubbing his jaw. "I know. I do. But you can't fall apart forever."

That was it. I didn't yell. I didn't throw the glass. I just left.

Grabbed my board from where it collected dust in the corner, slung my earbuds in, hoodie up, door slammed. I heard **Jax** call my name once. But I didn't stop.

Down the stairs, across the street, into the blur of **Floom City** at night—lit in flashes of purple and red neon, the hum of sky runners above, the scent of street noodles and damp metal. Music poured into my ears like armor.

Alien Blues by **Vundabar**. Volume up. World out.

I kicked off hard and let the wheels catch speed.

Faster.

The blur helped. The wind helped.

I was nothing but momentum, hoodie flapping, tears drying against the breeze before they even had a chance to matter.

But as I turned onto a cracked side street—empty, unlit, ignored by the city's tech grid—I felt it.

Eyes.

Someone watching.

I didn't slow down.

I should have.

Because the next second, something slammed into my shoulder—

A shove.

Hard.

Deliberate.

I flew off the sidewalk. My board shot sideways. My body tipped. I flailed—no balance, no grip—

And then I dropped.

Off the ledge.

Into darkness.

Toward something bubbling, blue, and alive.

PART 2

The Acid that Breathes

I didn't hit the ground. I hit something else. Thick. Wet. Cold. It swallowed me.

The moment my body broke through the surface, it was like being punched in every cell at once. I couldn't scream—my lungs locked up. The goo clung to my skin like static. It wasn't just a liquid. It moved. It reacted.

It breathed.

My limbs went numb. My ears rang. The world twisted into smears of blue and black and searing white pain. I tried to kick to the surface, but it was like swimming through rubber cement mixed with lightning.

I sank deeper.

Then—light.

Not from above.

From me.

I saw it.

My hands. My arms. My chest.

Glowing.

Thin cracks of light spiderwebbed beneath my skin, flickering like veins made of fire.

I opened my mouth to scream, and the liquid surged into my throat.

Then—

Darkness.

Stillness.

And then—

Heartbeat.

A single thud like thunder in my chest.

Then another.

Faster.

Louder.

Until it wasn't just my heart, it was everything.

I was burning.

Blue light pulsed outward in every direction, illuminating the walls of the alley, the edge of the cracked containment vat, the mossy bricks beyond.

Then—

I was yanked.

Out.

Up.

The world tilted.

A voice above me shouted. **Faint.**

Someone is grabbing my arm.

The last thing I saw before the world faded was a pair of hands pulling me out of the sludge, a flannel shirt sleeve, and the words, *"Hang in there, kid."*

Then nothing.

PART 3

The Glow that Shouldn't Be

The second hospital room in two months wasn't much of an upgrade.

Different building. Same off-white walls, same monitor beeps. The bed crinkled under me like a bag of chips every time I moved.

This time, two nurses were whispering outside the room. One of them kept looking at my chart as if it were written in another language.

Probably because it was.

None of it made sense.

My pulse had spiked and crashed three times overnight. My temperature dropped below safe levels, then surged to borderline fever. They'd tried three different thermometers before giving up.

But I felt... fine.

Well, not fine—more like, not dead. Which seemed impressive, considering what I'd landed in.

I sat up slowly, rubbing my eyes. Everything felt clearer. Sharper.

The hum of electricity in the wall. The tapping of a pen at the nurse's station. The buzz of a fly in the light fixture. I could hear it all.

My skin tingled, not like pins and needles—more like I was being charged from the inside.

The nurse stepped in and blinked when she saw me sitting up. "Oh. You're awake."

"Seems that way," I said.

She checked the monitor. It beeped erratically when she touched it.

"Weird," she muttered.

"What?"

"Machine says your heart rate's—" She paused, looked again. "Actually, never mind. I think it's just glitching."

I looked at the wires taped to my chest. They were warm.

Too warm.

She handed me a cup of water and left.

I took a sip, and as I set it down, the plastic cup hovered.

Not long.

Not high.

Just a whisper of lift—maybe half an inch off the tray.

Then it fell.

I stared at it.

My fingers pulsed blue again. Faint. Like static. Gone in a blink.

No one else saw.

But I did.

Something had changed.

PART 4

Unseen Flames

They discharged me that night.

Nurse **Joy** texted, relieved but brief: "We'll talk soon."

I didn't reply.

Jax was still out. I guessed he'd gone straight from the hospital to wherever he stored all that anxiety he didn't know what to do with. He always needed time after a scare—his own or mine.

The apartment felt smaller now, as if the walls had shifted inward just a few inches.

I sat on the edge of my bed, still wearing the sweats they gave me at the hospital. My fingers trembled when I looked at them too long.

Then I felt it again.

That hum.

Not around me—in me.

I stood up and took a breath. Deep. Focused. Stepped toward my skateboard, leaning against the wall.

"Okay," I muttered. "Just… test it."

I reached out a hand.

The board didn't move.

I furrowed my brow. Tried again.

Still nothing.

Then I closed my eyes—and let myself remember it.

The feeling of the acid. The weightless pull. The blue heat, crawling under my skin.

Something shifted.

A wind.

Inside the room.

I opened my eyes.

The board was *hovering* two inches off the floor.

Then it spun.

Slowly at first. Then faster, until the wheels buzzed like they were racing down a hill. I stepped back, heart hammering.

My breath caught in my throat.

And then—

"Callum."

The board dropped like a stone.

I spun around.

Jax stood in the doorway. No words. Just staring.

He'd seen it.

The board. The levitation. The fear on my face.

I swallowed hard. "I can explain."

"You'd better."

PART 5

The Push

The next day, **Jax** didn't speak to me.

Not in anger. Not in avoidance.

He obviously didn't know what to say, but

Neither did I.

He'd seen something no brother should have to process. He didn't ask questions, not yet—but I saw it in his eyes. Not fear. Not disappointment.

Worry.

Like I was slipping into something he couldn't reach.

By late afternoon, I needed air. Or movement. Or both.

So I told **Jax** I was "going for a walk." He nodded slowly, didn't look up from his tablet.

I took my board, pulled my hoodie up, and went back.

Back to that alley. The one that swallowed me whole.

It looked different in the daylight—smaller, almost normal. The fence was still half-collapsed, the pavement stained with something dried and black. The containment vat was gone, probably cleaned up, covered up, and forgotten.

But I hadn't forgotten.

I stood on the edge of the ledge, just above where I'd fallen, and tried to piece it together. The music. The shove. The fall.

And then—

"Looking for something?"

I spun around, almost tripping over my own feet.

He stood at the end of the alley.

Black hoodie. Boots. Calm. Confident.

Older than me, but not by much. Pale skin, sharp features. Eyes like cooled coal—gray with something burning beneath.

Cerces.

Even though I didn't know his name yet, I knew him.

The kind of person who didn't belong to any street or school or city—he owned whatever space he stepped into.

"You—" I started.

He tilted his head slightly, hands in his pockets. "Yes. Me."

"You pushed me."

"Correct."

"Why?"

He stepped forward, slow and casual, like we were just old friends catching up.

"Because someone needed to wake you up."

My jaw clenched. "You could've killed me."

"But I didn't," he said. "Impressive, right?"

I stared at him, trying to place his voice, his face, his everything.

There was no fear in him. No hesitation. As if he already knew how the scene would unfold.

He turned to leave.

"Wait—who are you?"

He stopped just long enough to glance over his shoulder.

"Think of me as the beginning of your story, **Callum.**"

Then he vanished.

No smoke. No sound.

Just heat in the air where he'd stood.

CHAPTER THREE

The Misfits

PART 1

Back to the Fire

It started with scorch marks.

They hadn't been there the last time.

Black streaks along the brick wall at the far end of the alley—jagged, uneven, like someone had dragged fire across the surface just for fun.

I stared at them, heart thudding louder than I liked. The light around me flickered, though there were no lamps nearby. No reason for shadows to dance the way they were.

Still, I came back the next day.

And the day after.

Maybe I wanted answers. Perhaps I wanted to prove to myself that **Cerces** had been real, not just some *hallucination* caused by a concussion and a stormy night's sleep.

Or maybe I wanted to see what came next.

By the third night, it wasn't just scorch marks.

There were whispers.

Not voices exactly—more like soundless thoughts brushing the edge of my mind. I couldn't make out words, but I felt the pull. Something beneath the pavement. Something just… below.

On the fifth night, I heard footsteps before I saw him.

Cerces walked into the alley like it belonged to him. Which, honestly, it probably did.

Same black hoodie. Same boots. Same measured pace, neither rushing nor hesitating.

"Persistent," he said, not looking at me. "I respect that."

I folded my arms. "You going to shove me into another chemical vat, or are we past that?"

He smiled—small, unreadable. "If I wanted you dead, **Callum**, you would be."

"Reassuring."

He stopped a few feet away. "You came back."

"You knew I would."

"I hoped you would," he corrected. "Hope is far more human."

I hesitated. "What do you want?"

"Not here," he said. "It's too loud."

"It's an abandoned alley."

He nodded once. "Exactly."

Then he turned and walked toward the back wall.

I almost stayed.

Almost let him disappear again.

But something in me buzzed—like a wire pulled taut.

So I followed.

PART 2

Underground

The wall opened.

Not like a door.

Like a trick.

Cerces touched a brick near the scorched corner, and the entire section shimmered, then split down the center with a hiss of steam. Behind it: a narrow stone staircase leading down into pitch black.

"No pressure," he said, glancing back at me. "You can turn around."

He knew I wouldn't.

So I followed.

The steps descended far deeper than I expected—past the foundation of the city, past where the noise of hovercars and nightlife faded into a low hum. The walls changed from brick to metal, then to something older—polished stone etched with glowing symbols I couldn't recognize.

The air grew warmer. Heavier.

Like we were walking into the throat of something alive.

At the bottom, a door slid open.

The space beyond looked nothing like what I'd imagined.

It wasn't dark or dungeon-like. It was massive. Lit in deep red and soft amber. The floors shimmered like obsidian[4] glass. Training platforms hovered in midair, pulsing with motion.

And everywhere—kids.

Teenagers like me, but not like me.

One hovered above the floor, arms crossed, suspended in midair—another hurled flame at a moving target, which exploded in sparks. A girl sprinted across the ceiling as if it were solid ground.

These were **The Misfits.**

And they weren't hiding.

---

[4]Obsidian: is a naturally occurring volcanic glass, typically black, formed from the rapid cooling of molten lava. Source: Google Definition.

Cerces stepped beside me. "You thought you were the only one."

I didn't answer.

"Everyone here," he continued, "survived something they shouldn't have. Fire. Poison. Death. Power finds survivors, **Callum**. It rewards them."

I looked at him. "So this is what? A club for weirdos with trauma?"

He smirked. "We prefer the term '*awakened*.'"

Someone walked by and nodded to **Cerces**—a tall kid with silver tattoos glowing under his skin.

They didn't speak, but the look between them was clear: respect. Obedience.

Cerces turned back to me. "Come. There's more."

I followed. Slowly. Trying not to show how fast my heart was beating.

PART 3

The Speech

We walked through the complex like ghosts—everyone saw us, but no one spoke. No one needed to.

Cerces moved like a general through a base he built himself. Every turn revealed something stranger than the last: a circular chamber filled with levitating stones; a library of floating tablets inscribed in languages I didn't recognize; a sparring room where two kids launched lightning at each other like it was a game of catch.

But none of it surprised me more than how calm he was.

Cerces didn't gloat or posture, nor did he try to impress me.

He just existed—entirely sure that I would eventually come around.

We stopped outside a chamber built of black stone and red glass.

He gestured for me to step inside.

The room was quieter. Cooler. A lounge, almost. A single couch, a table, dim lights overhead.

Cerces didn't sit; he just stood across from me.

"Callum," he said, "do you know what the world does to people like us?"

I didn't answer.

"It tries to control us. Dilute us. Medicate us. Make us feel guilty for surviving something most people never will."

He sauntered, like pacing thoughts into shape.

"But you didn't die, did you?" he continued. "You fell into something impossible. Something that should've torn you apart. And you came out changed."

He stopped in front of me.

"You think that was an accident?"

I shook my head. "I think it was horrifying."

"It was honest." His voice sharpened. "This city lies to you. Pretends to care. Pretends it'll protect you. But the second you don't fit the script, you get discarded. The Misfits? We rewrite the script."

I crossed my arms. "And what's your version?"

He stepped closer, voice low.

"Power. Control. Truth. You don't wait to be rescued. You become the force no one dares to cage."

Something was intoxicating in the way he said it. Not just the words—how certain he was.

For a second, I understood the kids training outside—the loyalty in their eyes.

But the chill running down my spine wasn't awe.

It was a warning.

PART 4

The Photo

Cerces turned to the glass coffee table in the center of the room and tapped it twice.

A ripple of light passed through the surface.

A single image appeared—flat, glowing faintly blue.

I stepped closer.

Dorian.

She was walking down the street, headphones on, mid-laugh. It wasn't just a snapshot. It was recent. Maybe a day or two old.

My stomach twisted.

"How did you—"

"I know everything about you, **Callum**," Cerces said,

calm as ever. "Everyone you care about. Everyone you protect."

I stared at the image. **Dorian** hadn't changed. Same half-braided hair, same chipped nail polish, same too-loud music, and unfiltered smile. She looked… safe.

And now, she wasn't.

"Are you threatening her?" I asked, jaw tight.

"No," Cerces said. "I'm warning you."

He tapped the image again. It vanished.

"If you don't understand what you are… if you refuse to learn… she pays the price."

I took a step forward. "You don't touch her."

He raised a hand, almost amused. "I wouldn't need to. The world already does. I'm offering you a chance to stop that. To stop anyone from ever being able to hurt what's yours."

The way he said it—what's yours—made my skin crawl.

"You think you're offering protection," I said. "But this? This is manipulation."

Cerces tilted his head, as if surprised I'd found the word.

He didn't argue.

Didn't need to.

Because deep down, I knew he was right about one thing.

I didn't know how to protect anyone.

Not yet.

PART 5

The Refusal

Cerces didn't ask again.

He didn't need to.

He just stood there, calm, patient, like someone waiting for a door to open on its own.

But I wasn't ready to walk through it.

"I'm not like you," I said.

His smile barely flickered. "Not yet."

"I don't want to hurt people."

He stepped forward, voice quiet but sharp. "You will."

The words hit like ice water.

Not a threat. A prediction.

"You don't have control," he continued. "You're a fuse. One spark away from burning everything you love. You think kindness protects people? It weakens them."

I stared at him.

"You sound like someone who used to believe in love," I said. "And got hurt enough to forget."

That made him pause.

Just for a second.

And then, as if nothing had happened, he extended a hand.

"Join us, **Callum**. You're already one of us. You survived what no one else could. That makes you a weapon. Learn how to wield yourself."

I looked at his hand.

It wasn't the fire that scared me.

It was how much of me wanted to take it.

But I didn't.

I stepped back.

"No."

He held my gaze, then slowly lowered his arm.

"No," he echoed, like he was trying on the word.

Then, with no flare or drama, he raised a finger and flicked it toward the air.

A swirl of heat spun around me—light and pressure and sound folding together—

And then I was back.

In my apartment.

Alone.

I staggered to the couch, barely catching myself.

The city buzzed outside the window like nothing had happened.

But I could still feel the warmth of his world on my skin.

Still hear his voice in my head.

Still see the blue light curling around my fingertips.

CHAPTER FOUR

The Gods

PART 1

The Blowout

I didn't want to go to school. That should've been the first sign.

But I went anyway, because pretending to be normal was easier than explaining why I wasn't.

The halls buzzed with their usual noise—hover-shoes skimming the tiles, conversations too loud, eyes that never really saw you. I kept my hoodie up, my head down.

Then I heard her voice.

"Callum."

Dorian.

I turned. **Dorian** was standing by my locker, arms crossed, eyebrows already raised like she was halfway through an argument.

"Where have you *been?*" she asked, no hello, no buildup. "You vanish for three days and show up like nothing happened?"

"I've been dealing with stuff," I muttered.

"Clearly. Your eyes glowed in math class yesterday."

I looked around. No one else seemed to notice.

"Dorian—"

"You lied to me." Her voice cracked. "You said everything was under control."

"I never said that."

"You let me believe it."

That hit harder than I wanted to admit.

"I didn't mean to—"

"Then what did you mean to do, **Callum?** Hide? Pretend nothing's changing? Because newsflash—*you're changing.* And not in the *good, Spider-Man gets a cool suit* kind of way. You're—"

"I *know* I'm messed up!" I snapped.

The air shifted.

Her ponytail fluttered.

Papers from a nearby locker rustled.

"**Callum**," she said slowly. "What did you just—"

I didn't mean to.

But she lifted off the floor.

Not high. Just a foot. Maybe two.

Her eyes widened, hair lifting like static, arms flailing slightly in panic.

"Stop it!" she shouted.

I panicked. My hands shot up—and she *flew* backward, slammed into a locker with a metallic thud.

She slid down to the floor, dazed, staring at me like I was something she didn't recognize.

"**Dorian**—I didn't—" I stepped forward.

"Don't," she said, standing up, breathing hard. "Don't come near me."

I froze.

Tears blurred her eyes, but she didn't let them fall.

"I don't know what you are anymore," she whispered. "But you're not the **Callum** I knew."

Then she walked away.

And I didn't stop her.

Because for the first time, I wasn't sure she was wrong.

PART 2

The Other Brother

I didn't go home.

Couldn't.

Jax would've asked questions, and I wasn't in the mood to lie with that much detail.

So I skated.

Hard.

Across streets I didn't know, through alleys I hadn't touched since before the acid, the burn, the *change*. The board hummed beneath me like it knew I needed the speed. The wind tore at my hoodie. My eyes stung.

I ended up where I always did.

The alley.

The place where I fell, where **Cerces** pushed, where it all began.

I stood there, breathing hard, waiting.

Nothing moved.

The scorch marks were gone now and scrubbed off. But I could still *feel* them—echoes in the brick, in the hum of the air, in my veins.

"Back again?"

The voice wasn't **Cerces**.

It was softer. Calmer.

I spun around, fists clenched.

He stood in the shadow between two buildings. Same build. Same age.

But he wasn't **Cerces**.

No smirk. No swagger. Just stillness.

He stepped into the light.

He looked like **Cerces** might've, if he slept. If he didn't carry a wildfire in his spine.

"You're not him," I said.

"No."

"Then who—"

"I'm **Crae**," he said. "His brother."

My mouth went dry.

"Twin, technically," he added. "Though I think I aged better."

I blinked. "Why are you here?"

Crae studied me for a long moment. "Because you're not just his mistake to fix. You're also someone else's responsibility to save."

"I don't need saving."

"You do," he said gently. "You just don't want it."

He turned, nodding toward a narrow side passage I'd never noticed before—a door opened at the end—silent, glowing gold from within.

"I'm not like him," **Crae** said without turning back. "I don't force people. I offer them a choice."

I hesitated.

"I just hurt the only person who's ever believed in me," I said. "I don't even know what I'm becoming."

Crae nodded. "Then it's time you learned."

He stepped into the light.

And I followed.

PART 3

The Golden Path

The tunnel sloped downward, but it wasn't dark.

Soft gold light pulsed along the floor like a heartbeat, warm and steady. The walls were stone, smooth but ancient, etched with delicate patterns I couldn't name—like veins, or constellations.

We walked in silence.

Crae didn't need to fill the space. His presence was calm, magnetic in the opposite way from **Cerces**. Where **Cerces** pulled you in like fire, **Crae** gave you room to breathe.

After what felt like forever, the tunnel opened.

And everything changed.

I stepped into a circular chamber, domed and glowing. White marble floors. Columns that shimmered faintly. Dozens of teens moved between open archways, sparring, reading, meditating.

No one yelled.

No one boasted.

No explosions or flaming fists.

Just motion. Focus.

Balance.

"Welcome to the Sanctuary," **Crae** said. "We call ourselves *The Gods*."

I raised an eyebrow. *"Subtle."*

He smirked. "It stands for *Generation of the Dominated*. Everyone here knows what it means to be crushed by something—grief, pain, power. We don't reject it. We master it."

A girl floated by on a platform of light, her hands weaving patterns in the air. Two others knelt at a long table, studying a glowing map of what looked like **Floom City**.

"Your brother's group... the **Misfits**," **Crae** continued. "They seek power to reshape the world in their image. We seek control *of ourselves first*. Then, if the time comes, the world."

He turned to face me.

"You've felt it, haven't you? The fear. The storm under your skin. You were never meant to carry that alone."

I didn't answer.

Because yes—I had.

And no—I didn't want to admit it.

Crae stepped aside and gestured to a quiet hallway lit in soft amber.

"If you want to train," he said, "we'll show you how. If you don't—no one will stop you."

He didn't say anything else.

He just walked away.

And left the door open behind him.

PART 4

The Offer Repeated

The room **Crae** led me to was nothing like **Cerces'** lair. It wasn't designed to impress. It didn't pulse with threat or ego. Just a single couch. A low black table. A gold line running along the floor like a boundary someone dared you to cross.

Crae motioned for me to sit.

I did, slowly. My shoulders ached like I'd been carrying something I couldn't name.

He sat across from me, posture perfect, hands folded loosely in his lap.

"We don't ask for loyalty," he said. "Not the way **Cerces** does."

"Then what *do* you ask for?"

"Purpose."

I scoffed before I could stop myself. "What makes you think I have one?"

"You wouldn't have survived if you didn't."

He said it like a fact, not flattery.

"You fell into the same acid my brother did," he continued. "It should have consumed you. But you didn't burn. You *adapted*. That's not by chance. That's by design."

"Design by who?"

Crae shrugged, but not in dismissal, more like acceptance. "We don't pretend to know all the answers. But we believe power without direction becomes destruction. And we've seen enough of that."

I thought of **Dorian**. Of her eyes, wide with fear. Of her silence as she walked away.

"I can't join you," I said. "I don't trust... anything right now. I   simply want to learn how to stop hurting people."

Crae nodded. "Then train. No strings. No vows. You help when you can. That's all we ask."

I looked at him.

He wasn't **Cerces**. He wasn't anyone I'd ever met.

He was a mirror held up to who I *could* be—if I stopped running.

I nodded.

"Alright," I said. "Show me where to start."

Crae stood.

And for the first time since the fall, the flame, the glow—

I didn't feel alone.

PART 5

The First Step

The training chamber wasn't flashy. No glowing targets. No floating platforms. Just an expansive circular room with soft lighting and walls that seemed to absorb sound. The kind of place built not for spectacle, but for focus.

Crae walked me to the center and stood in silence.

"First rule," he said. "Your powers aren't tricks. They're truths. Extensions of your soul. If your soul is fractured, so is your control."

"So I'm hopeless, then," I muttered.

He didn't smile. But he didn't disagree either.

"Second rule," he continued. "Fear isn't the enemy. It's the entry point. We don't teach you to *banish* it—we teach you to *listen.*"

I nodded, unsure whether I understood or was only pretending to do so.

He held out a small metal orb.[5]

"Focus on it," he said. "Don't move it. Don't lift it. Just feel it. Its weight. Its temperature. Its stillness."

I held out my hand. The orb hovered just above my palm.

I stared.

Nothing happened.

I waited.

Still nothing.

And then—Suddenly…

I heard it.

Not with my ears. With something deeper.

The faintest buzz. A thread connecting the orb to me.

---

[5] Orb — is generally something shaped like a ball of a sphere, which can refer to celestial bodies like the sun or moon, or the symbolic royal orb bearing a cross. Source: Google Definition.

I reached with my mind—not to control it, but to *know* it.

It trembled—just a little.

Crae nodded. "Good."

I exhaled, not even realizing I'd been holding my breath.

After training, **Crae** walked me back through the marble halls.

"You'll return here each morning," he said. "No one will come for you. You must choose it."

I nodded. "I will."

He stopped near a glowing sigil[6] on the wall and raised one hand.

A soft gust of wind swirled around us, and suddenly—

Home.

I stood in my bedroom again, quiet and dim.

But something had changed.

The wind from the portal still lingered—calm, golden, gentle.

---

[6] Sigil – a unique, custom-created symbol used in magic and other occult practices to represent a specific intention or desire. Source: Google Definition.

It curled around me as I stepped to the window.

And for the first time in weeks, it didn't burn.

It *glowed*.

CHAPTER FIVE

FEAR TRIGGER

PART 1

The Pattern

The morning came quietly, as if it knew I needed a break. No fire in the sky. No voices in my head. Just light through the curtains and the faint smell of leftover takeout.

I slipped on my hoodie, grabbed my board, and whispered a quick lie to **Jax** about heading to school. He didn't question it—maybe because he was too tired, or maybe because part of him knew I was doing something more important than algebra.

Crae met me at the same alley entrance. He didn't speak when I arrived. He just nodded and opened the portal with a simple wave of his hand. Gold light shimmered around us.

I stepped through.

The Sanctuary was quieter than usual. Some of the other trainees nodded as I passed, but none spoke. Not out of rudeness. Out of focus. Everyone here had their own storms to tame.

Crae waited for me in the center chamber, a polished obsidian disc beneath his feet, glowing lines curling outward like the spokes of a wheel.

Today, the room was darker. Not dim. Controlled. As if the walls had chosen a mood to match my head.

"We're changing the rhythm," Crae said without turning. "You've learned to move things. Now you learn when they move you."

I raised an eyebrow. "That sounds like something a yoga instructor would say before handing me a stress ball."

He smirked. "Good. You're still sarcastic. You'll need that."

He motioned to a floating orb that drifted slowly between us. This one was different—shifting colors, pulsing in time with something I couldn't hear.

"What is it?"

"It's tied to your emotional frequency. Watch."

He raised a hand. The orb turned red.

"**Anger,**" he said.

He stepped aside. It turned blue.

"**Calm.**"

Then he looked at me. "Now you."

I stepped forward, heart racing.

The orb flickered.

Orange. Yellow.

Then deep, flickering **blue.**

And suddenly—**crack.**

The stone under my feet fractured.

The glow around my fingers returned, brighter than ever.

"Fear," **Crae** said softly.

My breath caught. "I wasn't scared."

"You were." He stepped forward, voice even. "You're always scared. That's what makes you powerful."

I shook my head. "Fear is weakness."

"No," he said. "Fear is honesty. Power that responds to it isn't flawed—it's *true*. You don't need to destroy fear. You need to listen to it."

I stared at the glowing lines on my skin.

They pulsed with every beat of my heart.

"You're saying... fear is my trigger."

Crae nodded. "It always has been."

PART 2

Disrupted Frequencies

Dorian always said vending machines were scams wrapped in metal.

Today, she had proof.

It was after school, and she stood in front of the cracked, humming beast by the gym. Her soda had jammed halfway down the spiral coil and refused to fall.

"Unbelievable," she muttered. "I swear, if I had actual powers—"

Click.

The light inside the machine blinked once.

Then again.

And then, with a soft *bzzt*, the entire row of drinks dropped at once.

She stepped back, stunned, as the machine sputtered and spat out two extra bottles for good measure.

A faint current tickled her fingertips.

She looked down.

Nothing.

But she'd felt it—like static humming under her skin, like her own pulse wasn't quite synced to reality anymore.

This wasn't the first time.

Yesterday, she unplugged her phone from its charger, and it stayed at 100% all day. The day before that, every time she touched metal, it sparked. Not badly—just enough to make her flinch.

She told herself it was stress. The **Callum** stuff. The weirdness with the sky. Sleep deprivation.

But part of her didn't believe that anymore.

She sat on the curb outside school, clutching the extra soda bottles like trophies she hadn't earned.

Her phone buzzed.

A message from **Callum**: *"Hope you're okay."*

She stared at the screen.

Then locked it.

She wasn't ready to answer yet.

Not until she figured out what was happening to her.

PART 3

Friction

The *orb* didn't move.

For the third time in a row, it hovered just outside my reach—silent, neutral, refusing to react.

I clenched my jaw and pushed harder, trying to summon the spark, the pressure, the *something* that usually rose when I needed it.

Nothing.

Across the room, **Crae** watched silently.

I turned away from the *orb* and kicked at the floor. My boot scraped against the marble with a sound like frustration made solid.

"This is pointless," I muttered.

"Because you didn't lift it?"

"Because I don't know who I'm becoming," I snapped. "I don't even know who I *was* before all this. I can't go back, and I don't know how to go forward."

Crae stepped closer.

"You're not here to go back."

I looked up at him. "You ever feel like you're the result of a mistake that didn't kill you? Like the world meant to erase you, but it missed?"

He was quiet for a moment.

Then: "Maybe you're not the mistake. Maybe you're the correction."

I blinked.

"That's the thing about surviving," he continued. "It feels like an accident. But sometimes, it's a blueprint. You're not broken, **Callum**. You're unfinished."

I looked down at my hands. The faintest threads of blue shimmered just beneath the skin—barely there, like breath on glass.

"You believe that?" I asked.

Crae nodded once. "I have to. I've seen what happens to people who don't."

For the first time, I let the silence settle without fighting it.

And this time, it didn't feel like a weight.

It felt like space.

PART 4

Return of the Flame

It was past midnight when it happened.

The apartment was dark, quiet, and still. **Jax** was out late—on the night shift again. I sat at my desk, sketching on the back of an old math worksheet. I wasn't drawing anything in particular—just shapes. Flame-shaped ones.

A soft *click* echoed behind me.

Then a hiss.

I turned.

My living room light was on.

But I hadn't touched it.

And then it changed—flickering—not with electricity, but *fire*.

The air shimmered. The shadows on the walls stretched too long, too tall.

And there he was.

Cerces.

Or rather—a projection of him. His body flickered in orange flame, hovering just above the floor, eyes molten, voice thick with smoke.

"You're improving," he said, smiling faintly. "It's adorable."

I stood slowly. **"Get out."**

"This isn't your apartment," he said. "This is your *threshold*. Every place you think is safe is just a waiting room for truth."

"You're not real," I said.

He tilted his head. "Then why are you shaking?"

I looked down.

My hands were glowing again.

Not like before.

Brighter.

Hotter.

"You've tried their path," **Cerces** said. "The soft one. The still one. Tell me—has it put out the fire? Or has it made you better at *hiding* it?"

I clenched my fists. "What do you want?"

He leaned in, voice low. "To remind you: balance is a myth. You don't get to live in between. Sooner or later, the world will make you choose."

The flames flared, swallowing him whole.

And then he was gone.

I stood in the silence, sweat on my neck, breath sharp in my chest.

Behind me, the page I'd been sketching on curled at the corners—singed.

Just enough to blur the lines.

PART 5

A Spark of Her Own

Dorian dreamed of lightning.

Not the kind that cracks and vanishes.

The kind that *lingers*.

She stood in a field of stars—each one pulsing to her heartbeat. Her hands glowed white. Her feet hovered just above the ground.

The sky split open above her.

And through it, a voice:

"You are not lost. You are seen."

She jolted awake.

Breath hitched. Hands trembling.

And glowing.

Not blue.

Gold.

Tiny arcs of electricity danced between her fingertips—silent, clean, impossibly bright. Her bedroom glowed like a lantern, and every device in the room blinked in quiet reverence.

The alarm clock blinked 2:46.

The metal lamp on her desk sparked, then melted softly at the base.

She covered her hands instinctively—like she could hide light by holding it tighter.

But it didn't go away.

It hummed through her skin. Warm. Alive.

Across the street, in his own dark apartment, **Callum** stood at his window.

He wasn't looking for signs.

But he saw one anyway.

Dorian's window lit up like morning.

Just for a second.

Then dark again.

But not before he caught the shape of her—standing there, arms out, haloed in light.

His breath caught.

Not from fear.

From awe.

She was like him now.

And maybe, just maybe, that meant he wasn't alone.

CHAPTER SIX

The Challenge

PART 1

Game On

The morning came with silence.

Too much of it. I woke up already sweating, like my body knew something before my brain caught up.

The sun hadn't risen yet. The sky outside my window was pale gray, neither night nor morning. My room looked dim and unfamiliar, like it had been rearranged in my sleep.

Then my phone buzzed.

Just once.

No sound. No caller ID.

The screen lit up white, then red.

A video loaded automatically.

My breath stopped.

It was **Dorian.**

Bound to a chair. Chains—not metal, but glowing. Writhing. Alive.

Her mouth was gagged with light.

Her eyes found the camera—and I could see the terror there. But also fury. She hadn't given up. Not even close.

Then the camera shifted.

Cerces.

Calm as ever. That wolf-smile stretched across his face.

"Morning, little ember," he said, voice clear in my room despite the phone's tiny speakers. "She was harder to catch than expected. But we always get what we want."

He crouched beside **Dorian,** eyes gleaming.

"She's strong," he said. "Brighter than we thought. So here's the game."

He held up three fingers.

"Three hours. That's how long you have to find us. After that, I teach her how to burn."

My heart thudded.

He winked. "And if you come with help, I erase her."

The screen went black.

Then: 00:00:00

And a timer began.

I dropped the phone.

It kept counting.

Three hours.

PART 2

The Strategy

The moment the timer started, I ran.

Didn't grab my board.

Didn't text **Jax**.

Didn't breathe.

Just ran.

The alley answered.

Crae was already waiting, standing by the wall like the tension in the air had summoned him.

I didn't waste time.

"He has her," I said. "**Dorian**. Chains. Some magical gag. Three-hour clock."

Crae didn't blink. "Show me."

I held out my phone. The screen still pulsed with the countdown: 02:42:16.

He tapped the air above it once.

A shimmer peeled off the screen—like heat rising—and hovered in midair.

"Echo signature," he murmured. "Fire-based, but unstable."

"**Cerces**," I said.

Crae nodded. "But he's not alone. That's binding, that's dragon script. **Arimaeus**."

My stomach dropped. "**The Dragon Emperor?**"

Crae turned, already walking. "They're in one of the Underspines—abandoned tunnels beneath the city. But there's only one that resonates with fire *and* fear."

I followed. "You've been there?"

"Once," he said. "I barely got out."

We reached the portal chamber. **Crae** raised both palms to the air. A long, low tone echoed through the floor. A golden ring appeared, flickering at the edges.

"This is a one-way door," he warned. "Once we're in, we don't pop back out."

"What's the plan?"

Crae looked at me.

"You extract **Dorian**. I engage **Cerces**."

I shook my head. "That's a death match."

"Only if we lose," he said.

And then the portal swallowed us.

PART 3

The Extraction

The Underspines smelled like ash and old metal.

Walls pulsed with red veins—alive but dying, like bloodlines made of fire.

Crae and I moved in silence, boots echoing down narrow tunnels. He walked ahead, blade in hand—not a sword exactly, but a length of glowing metal curved like a crescent moon.

The deeper we went, the hotter it got.

Then we heard it.

A hum.

Not mechanical.

Musical.

Cerces was singing.

His voice bounced off the stone, lazy and amused.

" 🎵 Red light, bright light, sing until it's gone... 🎵 "

Crae's expression didn't change. "He's close."

We split at the fork—his path curved toward the main chamber.

Mine dipped low, toward a side vault.

I crept forward.

There she was.

Dorian, chained to a pillar of obsidian. Coils of light locked her arms, her mouth covered by a soft-glowing mask.

She wasn't unconscious.

Her eyes met mine instantly.

And there was *rage* in them.

I knelt beside her, whispering. "It's me. I'm gonna get you out."

She nodded once—sharp.

The chains buzzed with energy. I reached for them, unsure how to—

Then I remembered.

Fear is your trigger.

I closed my eyes.

Focused not on the chains but on the fear of losing her.

The energy surged through me. Not explosive. Directed.

The chains snapped.

The gag burned off in a ripple of sparks.

She gasped. "He's still here. He's—"

"**Crae's** keeping him busy."

She stood—barefoot, hair wild, eyes glowing *faintly*.

Not blue.

Not gold.

Something in between.

"I feel… *different*," she said.

"You look it," I said. "Can you walk?"

She held up one hand. Lightning crackled in her palm.

"I can *run*."

PART 4

The Reveal

The escape didn't last long.

We hit the upper tunnel, moving fast—**Dorian**'s lightning lighting the path, our feet pounding against stone.

Then the light *stopped*.

And the heat hit.

Cerces stood at the end of the passage, arms folded, flames curling around his boots.

Crae was nowhere in sight.

"Running?" **Cerces** asked. "That's cute."

Dorian raised her hands, lightning dancing between her fingers. "One more step and I'll light you up."

He smiled like that was the most romantic threat he'd ever heard.

But his eyes flicked to me.

"This is the moment, you know," Cerces said. "The one where he chooses."

"What are you talking about?" I asked.

He stepped forward, voice low and certain.

"You think you were born to chaos. But you weren't."

A flick of his hand—and fire erupted across the ceiling in a ring of symbols.

Hades' mark.

"You were *sent*," he said.

I blinked. "No—no, that's not—"

"You survived the acid because it *knew* you. It recognized its own. You aren't just powered, **Callum.** You're legacy. You're *mine.*"

"No," I said again, staggering back.

"You are the Son of Hades," Cerces said. "And that power inside you? It's not a mutation. It's a birthright."

Dorian reached for my hand.

I didn't move.

Not because I didn't want to.

Because I couldn't feel my legs.

The fire—the fear—it all made sense now.

And none of it felt like mine.

PART 5

The Escape

Cerces didn't wait for a reaction.

He raised both hands, and the tunnel shook.

The walls ignited—black stone fracturing, veins of fire lashing out like serpents. **Dorian** pulled me back, but I barely felt her hand. My ears rang with the same word, over and over:

Hades.

Crae burst in through the side wall, his blade spinning in a loop of gold. Fire met it—and scattered.

He shouted something, but I couldn't hear.

Dorian grabbed my shoulder, lightning surging through her arm. "Snap out of it!"

I blinked.

The flame retreated from my skin—not gone, but *called back.*

Cerces was no longer a man.

He rose into the tunnel's dome, body elongating, skin splitting into plates of obsidian and ash. Wings of fire erupted from his back.

His voice, now layered with something more profound, echoed through the stone:

"You'll see soon. The fire *always* claims its heir."

Crae spun his blade and drove it into the floor.

A rip in the air tore open behind us—pure gold light, unstable, shrinking.

"Go!" he shouted.

Dorian grabbed my hand and pulled me through.

The last thing I saw was **Cerces**, fully aflame, wings spread; and **Crae**, standing his ground.

Then: light.

Heat.

Cold.

Darkness.

And the echo of a truth I wasn't ready to own.

CHAPTER SEVEN

Revelations

PART 1

The Realm of Scrolls

We landed on glass.

Not real glass—something stronger. Something that pulsed with every step.

The space around us was endless, curving up into a dome with no ceiling. Walls of light flickered with language I couldn't read. Symbols moved like constellations across the surface. Every breath echoed as if it were being recorded.

Dorian stood beside me, arms still crackling faintly with golden sparks.

"**Where... are we?**" she whispered.

I opened my mouth to answer.

Nothing came.

A voice responded from above, everywhere and nowhere at once.

"You stand within the Realm of Scrolls."

The floor shifted beneath us, rearranging itself like puzzle pieces. Stairs unfolded, leading downward toward a single column of golden fire.

From it emerged a figure.

Tall. Robed in white and bronze. Face hidden beneath a hood that shimmered like starlight.

"I am **Keeper**," the voice said—not through lips, but through air itself.

Callum: "We don't have time for riddles. My friend—**Crae**—he's still fighting **Cerces**—"

The **Keeper** raised a hand.

A floating pane of light appeared.

It showed **Crae**—alive, surrounded by fire, deflecting blast after blast with radiant calm.

"He holds," the **Keeper** said. "But not forever."

Dorian stepped forward. "We need answers."

The **Keeper** turned to her.

"You are the **Daughter of Sky**," it said. "The bloodline of **Olympus** flows in your breath."

I turned sharply. "What?"

The **Keeper** turned to me.

"And you," it said. "**Son of Hades**. The fire beneath all fire. The balance must be restored."

Then the stairs parted.

Revealing a glowing scroll at the base of the flame.

Callum stepped forward.

And the truth began to write itself in light.

PART 2

The Language of Gods

The scroll hovered midair, its surface aglow with lines that pulsed like veins. Words bloomed across it—not in ink, but in threads of light.

I couldn't read them.

But **Dorian** could.

She stepped closer, eyes wide, lips parting unconsciously.

"I... I know this," she whispered. "I don't know how, but I do."

The **Keeper** nodded. "The tongue of **Olympus** lives in your blood."

She read slowly. The glowing text echoed with each syllable, the chamber humming in response.

"When flame and thunder share one sky," she read, "the

veil shall burn, and balance rise. The fallen heir of dark shall wake, The chosen spark, her bond shall make. Together, not alone, they stand— To heal or break the gods' command."

I stared at her.

"You're the spark," I said.

She looked at me. "And you're the fallen heir."

The words felt too big, like they belonged in a book, not our mouths.

But they weren't wrong.

Dorian reached out, brushing her fingers along the scroll's edge.

It flared briefly—bright gold and deep blue.

Opposite powers.

One flame.

"They meant for us to find this," she said.

I nodded, the truth settling like fire in my bones.

"And now **Cerces** wants to destroy it."

"No," the **Keeper** said, voice calm. "He wants to fulfill

it—in his image."

I turned back to the scroll.

And for the first time, I saw not a curse but a calling.

PART 3

A Hard Truth

We sat in the echo of the scroll, its light dimmed now, the prophecy still burning behind our eyes.

Dorian paced. I didn't.

I sat still.

Too still.

It was the stillness of someone holding their breath under an ocean.

"That prophecy doesn't say I save anything," I muttered. "It says I wake. That I might break everything."

"You heard the end," **Dorian** said. "To heal or break. It's a choice."

"Yeah?" I looked up. "And what if I've already broken

too much?"

She stopped pacing.

Then sat beside me.

"You remember the vending machine?" she said, quietly.

I blinked. "What?"

"The day it exploded," she said, smiling faintly. "I was so mad. So scared. Thought I was cursed. But now maybe that was the first time I lit up."

She met my eyes.

"You're not the only one who's scared of what's inside them."

I didn't speak.

But I listened.

Then footsteps.

Crae!

Singed, exhausted, but whole.

He approached slowly, his usual calm cracking just slightly around the edges.

"I failed to contain him," he said. "But I stalled him long enough for this."

He looked at the scroll.

Then back at us.

"I owe you a truth."

We waited.

"My power," he said. "It doesn't come from fire or combat or control."

He held out his hand. A petal of light appeared, hovered, and dissolved.

"I descend from **Aphrodite**."

Dorian blinked. "You're serious?"

He nodded. "And **Cerces** is what happens when love is twisted into possession."

I looked down at my hands.

"What does that make me?" I asked.

Crae's voice softened. "Someone born of death… with the power to choose life."

And for the first time, that sounded possible.

PART 4

The Choice

Later, I found myself standing at the edge of the scroll chamber, staring into the infinite white.

The sky here didn't move.

It didn't need to.

Everything felt paused, waiting on me to make the next move.

I gripped the edge of the ledge, heart pounding.

Run.

That voice again.

The one that always offered me exits when I needed courage.

Just walk away. Let them finish the war without you.

I closed my eyes.

I could see it—my escape. Faking normal. Quiet school days. Avoiding mirrors and never lighting up again.

But it wasn't real.

Not anymore.

Behind me, **Dorian** padded into the space between the silence and my thoughts.

"You don't have to save the world," she said softly. "But you can help me save *ours*."

I turned.

She didn't glow this time.

She didn't need to.

She *burned* with clarity.

I took a breath, and the flame inside me answered—not violently.

Willingly.

"We do this," I said.

Dorian nodded.

Crae joined us a moment later, shoulders squared.

"The veil is thinning," he said. "**Cerces** is preparing for something larger than himself. A ritual. A tear between worlds."

I raised an eyebrow. "And we can stop that?"

He didn't answer right away.

Then: "If you step into who you are—yes."

Dorian reached out.

I took her hand.

And for the first time, our powers didn't clash.

They braided.

PART 5

Back to Floom

The Realm of Scrolls didn't have doors.

It had *endings*.

Moments where you stopped asking questions and started writing answers.

Crae stepped forward, drawing a spiral of light in the air. It shimmered, then cracked open like glass splitting underwater. Through it, we saw **Floom**.

Not the **Floom** we knew.

This sky churned. Clouds moved in unnatural ways—pulled in a circle above the city's core. Fire flickered in the distance. Alarms echoed faintly, carried on wind that smelled like ozone and smoke.

Dorian gripped my hand tighter.

"Is it starting?" she asked.

Crae's jaw tightened. "He's tearing a gate. A full rift to the Dragon Realm. Once it opens, this world won't be enough to hold him."

"And we stop it," I said—not as a question.

Crae looked at me—not the boy who fell, or the one who hid—but the one who finally stood.

"We try."

He turned to the light.

"Just know," he added, "if we step through... there's no turning back."

Dorian looked at me.

I nodded.

She stepped forward.

So did I.

The light swallowed us whole.

And behind us, the Realm of Scrolls faded into silence— its prophecy fulfilled not in fire, but in footsteps.

CHAPTER EIGHT

The Banishment Ritual

PART 1

The Fall of the City

The first thing I felt was heat.

Not the comforting warmth I'd come to control—but the *wrong* kind. Suffocating. Sick.

Floom was on fire.

We stood at the edge of a rooftop, overlooking downtown. Plumes of black smoke curled into the sky like claws. Buildings burned at their centers—slowly, deliberately, like they were being *undone* from within.

Above it all, the clouds swirled in a spiraling ring, glowing red at the center.

That was where he was.

Crae scanned the horizon, lips pressed in a line. "He's using the city as fuel."

I couldn't look away. Sirens blared faintly below. People ran in the streets—tiny shapes in chaos. But some didn't run.

Some just stood.

Watching the sky.

Spellbound.

"What's happening to them?" **Dorian** asked.

Crae's voice was grim. "They're seeing what he wants them to see. Power without cost."

I clenched my fists. The fire inside me stirred—not in fear, not even in anger.

In *readiness*.

"Then we give them something else to believe in," I said.

Crae nodded once.

"We split," he said. "I'll move through the east blocks—evacuate as many as I can. **Dorian**, you move north. Stabilize the hospitals. **Callum**—"

"I go straight to him."

Crae hesitated. Then: "Not to win. To distract. Long

enough for the ritual."

I met his eyes. "I know."

We turned.

And ran into the burning city—

—not to save ourselves.

But to *stand* where no one else could.

PART 2

Dragonfire

I climbed the tower without thinking.

Every stair groaned under my weight. Heat pressed in from all sides, like the building itself was sweating. Above, the sky cracked—each lightning bolt a ribbon of red instead of white.

At the top: wind.

And flame.

I pushed the final door open—and stepped onto the roof.

There he was.

Not a man.

Not anymore.

Cerces crouched in the center of a scorched helipad, wings spread wide. His form towered over the buildings around him—scales of obsidian, claws like glass daggers, fire leaking from between plated jaws.

He turned his head slowly, eyes burning embers.

"Hello, heir," he said.

His voice was layered now. Metal scraping beneath velvet.

I stepped forward.

"I'm not yours."

"You *were*." He stretched, rising to full height. "You *are*. The only reason you lived. The only reason the flame chose you was me."

I didn't answer.

Didn't flinch.

He lowered his head. Smoke curled from his nostrils.

"Do you feel it?" he asked. "The pulse under the city? The tear forming? When the gate opens, we will not be gods. We will be *beyond* them."

"You mean destruction."

"I mean *clarity,*" he growled.

I lifted my hand.

The blue glow lit the rooftop.

And for the first time, he stepped back.

"You'd use it against me?" he asked. "Your own blood?"

"No," I said. "I use it *for* them."

And then—

We clashed.

PART 3

The Crown of Fire

Our powers met midair—his flame, my light.

The rooftop trembled.

Cerces roared, wings flaring as fire spun around him in cyclones. He rose off the ground, talons scraping sparks from concrete, tail whipping through a steel antenna like it was paper.

I stood still.

Hands glowing.

Heart steady.

Not calm.

Certain.

Crae's voice echoed in my head: *"Your origin doesn't define your ending."*

I drew a circle with my foot, just like he taught me.

Knelt.

And began the chant.

The language of the gods wasn't something I knew.

It was something I *remembered*.

It poured from my throat like heat—deep, ancient, undeniable.

Symbols flared beneath me in rings of blue and white flame.

Cerces hissed.

"What are you doing?" he snarled, flying higher, circling now. "You *can't*."

But I didn't stop.

The city below went quiet.

The wind calmed.

Even the fire paused, like it wanted to listen.

The circle grew brighter. The words came faster.

Then—

A crown of flame bloomed above my head.

Not his kind of fire.

Mine.

Gold. Blue. Flickering with purpose.

Cerces dove.

Too late.

The ritual had begun.

And I had become the center of it.

PART 4

The Rift Opens

The final word left my mouth like thunder.

The sky split.

Not just above the tower—but *everywhere*.

A line of gold light tore across the clouds, wide and jagged. From its center spilled a storm of ash and stars—swirling in slow motion, revealing a world beyond ours.

Not sky.

Not space.

A *realm*.

Mountains suspended in flame. Oceans of smoke. A colossal throne carved from bones and glass.

At its center:

Arimaeus.

The Dragon Emperor.

His form towered beyond imagination—wings curled like continents, eyes twin stars. His voice boomed across both worlds without sound:

"You call. I answer."

Cerces lifted his head—staring upward like a child glimpsing a long-lost father.

"Finally…" he whispered.

But the ritual was *my* voice now.

My power.

The crown on my head flared white-blue.

I screamed the last phrase—not in fear.

In finality.

The rift buckled.

Cerces lunged, wings flailing.

The circle beneath me expanded—wrapped him in chains of light.

But he didn't fight.

He laughed.

"You banish me?" he said. "Then I drag *you* with me."

He clawed through the air.

One talon—hooked in my chest.

And the rift opened wider.

PART 5

The Sacrifice

The talon pierced just enough.

Not blood.

But connection.

I felt his mind—hot, vast, unhinged—pressing against mine like a furnace trying to wear a mask.

He grinned, even as the ritual chains tightened. "If I fall," he whispered, "you fall too."

"No," I said, voice steady.

"I *drag* you," he corrected.

And then I made the choice.

I grabbed his claw, yanked myself forward, and locked eyes with him.

And pushed.

Not with rage.

Not with hate.

With *resolve*.

"You don't drag me," I said.

"I throw you."

With one final shout, I summoned every drop of power left in me.

Light exploded from my hands.

Cerces howled—not in pain, but in shock—as the circle snapped shut like a bear trap.

He vanished into the rift.

So did I.

The world went white.

Then black.

Then—

still.

No wind.

No pain.

Just—

quiet.

CHAPTER NINE

Where I Belong

PART 1

The Wish

The city was quiet now.

Not peaceful.

Just stunned.

Smoke drifted in lazy spirals over the rooftops. Streets glowed faintly with the remains of magical flame, but the chaos had stilled. The rift was gone. The storm had ended.

And so had he.

Dorian stood on the edge of the tower, where **Callum** had vanished.

The circle of scorched stone was still there—silent, cold, unbroken.

She didn't cry.

Not yet.

Her body shook too hard to allow it.

Crae stood a few steps behind her, arms crossed, face unreadable.

"He made the choice," he said softly.

"I didn't ask him to," she whispered.

"He didn't need permission."

The wind picked up, curling her hair around her face. She stared at the empty sky, every nerve in her body still crackling from the storm.

Then something inside her snapped.

Or *opened*.

She didn't scream.

Didn't fall to her knees.

Instead—

She raised her hands.

They glowed.

Brighter than ever.

Gold. White. Sharp.

The wind stopped, reversed, and centered around her like a cyclone held by silence.

She didn't think.

She just *felt*.

And then she whispered:

"Bring him back… to where he belongs."

The light flared—

And the world blinked.

PART 2

The Misfire

I woke in blue.

Not sky.

Not water.

Just—blue.

Everything shimmered like flame frozen in glass—soft, weightless. I lay on a field that wasn't a field. No grass. No ground. Just texture made of light.

I sat up.

No pain.

No sound.

Then—a step.

Someone approached.

Bare feet. Long robe. A presence that filled the space without sound.

Hades.

I knew him before he spoke.

Not because of fire or crowns or theatrics.

Because he looked at me the way no one else ever had—like he already knew me.

"Welcome," he said, voice like a funeral whispered by the stars.

I stood. "Am I dead?"

"Not exactly."

I blinked. "Then what *exactly* am I?"

He stepped closer. "You are where you belong. For now."

A second figure emerged from the haze.

Shorter.

Slighter.

Jax.

Not his body.

But something of him—something *whole*.

I staggered back. "No... I saw—"

Hades raised a hand. "What you saw was not the end. What you see now is not the beginning. This is between."

I turned, overwhelmed.

"This isn't right," I said. "**Dorian—Crae**—they're still fighting—"

"They are alive," he said. "Because *you* chose to fall."

My fists clenched. "Then send me back."

"I cannot."

"But—"

He touched my shoulder.

A pulse ran through me.

And I remembered **Dorian's** voice.

Not a scream.

A *wish.*

PART 3

Understanding

Hades sat beside me.

No throne.

No crown.

Just a man with eyes that didn't blink and hands that never moved unless they needed to.

"You think your story was about power," he said.

I didn't respond.

"But it was never about that. It was about the *place*. About knowing you weren't a mistake."

I stared ahead. The field of blue shimmered, endless.

"I was afraid," I whispered. "Every day. Even when I fought."

"That fear," he said, "was honest. Most gods forget it. You didn't."

I turned to him.

"You gave me this fire?"

"No," he said. "You *are* the fire."

He raised one hand.

A sphere of light hovered between his fingers—pure, pulsing, raw.

"This was placed in you before the fall. Before the acid. Before the pain. The world tried to erase you. But fire *remembers*."

I leaned closer.

"What happens now?"

"You decide," he said. "Return… or remain."

"Can I go back?"

He looked at me—really looked.

"That depends," he said, "on how much you want to *belong*."

I stood.

And for the first time, I didn't feel afraid.

I felt *ready*.

PART 4

The Spark Returns

The city had stopped burning.

But it hadn't healed.

Dorian stood at her bedroom window, arms crossed, face lit only by the dim glow of streetlamps below.

She hadn't changed clothes.

Hadn't moved much at all.

Crae had offered words.

She didn't remember any of them.

Only one thing mattered:

He was gone.

And she'd made the wish.

Not a chant.

Not a spell.

Just seven words whispered like a promise.

Bring him back to where he belongs.

But he didn't come back.

At least, not *here*.

A breeze slipped through the open window.

Then—

a flicker.

Tiny.

Blue.

It hovered just above her desk, no bigger than a candle flame. But it moved like it knew her.

She stepped closer, breath caught in her chest.

The flame pulsed once.

Twice.

Then curled upward—like a hand waving.

And vanished.

She stared at the space where it had been.

Then, finally—

She smiled.

PART 5

The Last Word

Somewhere between worlds, I walked.

No longer lost.

No longer hiding.

Just walking.

The light around me wasn't fire anymore.

It was a memory.

And I could feel her voice—**Dorian's**—still echoing in the choice she made.

I wasn't back.

But I wasn't gone.

And for the first time, that was enough.

Because now I knew the truth.

My voice, soft and steady, filled the space beyond silence:

"Maybe I wasn't left behind."

"Maybe I was planted."

"And maybe… just maybe…"

"The fire wasn't meant to consume me."

"It was meant to wake me up."

THE END

To the Reader

Dear Reader,

If you've come this far, then you know this story was never just about fire or gods or battles.

It was about belonging.

It was about being seen, even when you feel invisible. About holding onto light even when everything inside you feels dark. About knowing you are not a mistake—not your pain, not your story, not your survival.

God still sees you.

You are here for a reason.

Just like Callum.

Just like Dorian.

And maybe those flames you've been through? They didn't burn you because they were never meant to destroy you. They were meant to reveal what was already inside you—a spark that won't go out.

Here are the promises I held close while writing this:

➢ You are not alone. ~(Psalm 34:18)

➢ You were created with a purpose. ~(Jeremiah 29:11)

- ➢ You are stronger than fear.~(2 Timothy 1:7)

- ➢ You are being shaped by more than your scars.~(Romans 8:28)

- ➢ You will walk through the fire—and you will come out alive.~(Isaiah 43:2)

With love,

Keona King

ABOUT THE AUTHOR

Keona King *is a dedicated and compassionate high school student currently living in Mechanicsville, Maryland. Keona balances academic excellence with creative and community pursuits. She has a passion for storytelling, service, and reminding others that they're never alone. She loves painting and writing. When she's not working backstage as a stage manager for her school's theater productions, you can probably find her on the soccer field, helping out at her church, or volunteering with local nonprofits that support families in need.* Keona *brings heart and determination to everything she does.*

She's completed over 75 hours of community service, including hands-on projects - rebuilt homes with the **Appalachia Service Project***, contributed to public health efforts through an international medical internship where she helped diagnose and support care for a real patient in* **Nigeria***, and brought smiles to families in need through her work with*

*the **Caritas Resource Center** and **The Giving Closet**. Her work in the community reflects the same core values that shape her writing: hope, purpose, and the power of choosing light, especially in dark places.*

*She believes in using her time and creativity to make the world a little better, one act of kindness (or story) at a time. Her passion for uplifting others and giving voice to quiet strength shines through in **Generation of the Gods**, her debut novel. Inspired by faith, grounded in purpose, and written to encourage young readers to find hope in hardship, **Generation of the Gods** is a story about identity, power, purpose, and learning that you're not an accident. Through every page, she hopes readers discover what she's come to believe for herself: You're not here by accident. You're here for something bigger; your world needs you because you matter.*